Star-Bubble
Trouble

Little Wings
3

Star-Bubble Trouble

by Cecilia Galante
illustrated by Kristi Valiant

A STEPPING STONE BOOK™

Random House New York

For Mrs. Lyons's second-grade class—
the best teacher and kids in the world! —C.G.

For Rhiannon and Kennedy,
two wonderful big sisters. —K.V.

Text copyright © 2012 by Cecilia Galante
Cover art and interior illustrations copyright © 2012 by Kristi Valiant

Visit us on the Web!
SteppingStonesBooks.com
randomhouse.com/kids

Educators and librarians, for a variety of teaching tools, visit us at
randomhouse.com/teachers

Library of Congress Cataloging-in-Publication Data
Galante, Cecilia.
Star-bubble trouble / by Cecilia Galante ; illustrated by Kristi Valiant.
p.   cm. — (Little wings ; #3)
"A Stepping Stone Book."
Summary: While on her first school "cloud trip," young cupid Willa Bean tries to get a replacement for her baby brother's lost ball but makes some big mistakes that nearly spoil everyone's fun.
ISBN 978-0-375-86949-5 (pbk.) — ISBN 978-0-375-96949-2 (lib. bdg.) —
ISBN 978-0-375-98354-2 (ebook)
[1. Behavior—Fiction. 2. School field trips—Fiction. 3. Lost and found possessions—Fiction. 4. Brothers and sisters—Fiction. 5. Cupid (Roman deity)—Fiction.]
I. Valiant, Kristi, ill. II. Title.
PZ7.G12965St 2012 [Fic]—dc23 2011021884

Printed in the United States of America

10 9 8 7 6 5 4 3 2 1

Contents

Willa Bean's World

Willa Bean Skylight is a cupid. Cupids live in a faraway place called Nimbus, which sits just alongside the North Star, in a tiny pocket of the Milky Way. Nimbus is made up of three white stars and nine clouds, all connected by feather bridges. It has a Cupid Academy, where cupids go to school, a garden cloud, where they grow and store their food, and lots and lots of playgrounds.

Willa Bean lives on Cloud Four with her mother and father, her big sister, Ariel, and her baby brother, Louie. Cloud Four is soft and green. The air around it smells like rain and pineapples. Best of all, Willa Bean's best friend, Harper, also lives on Cloud Four, just a few cloudbumps away.

When cupids are ready, they are given special Earth tasks. That means they have to fly down to Earth to help someone who is having a hard time. Big cupids, like Willa Bean's parents, help Earth grown-ups with things like falling in love. Little cupids, like Willa Bean, help Earth kids if they feel mad, sad, or just plain stuck. Working with Earth people is the most important job a cupid has. It can be hard work, too, but there's nothing that Willa Bean would rather do.

Are you ready for a peek into Willa Bean's world? It's just a few cloudbumps away, so let's go!

Chapter 1

Babies Are a Disaster!

Willa Bean flapped her bright purple wings a little harder. "Snooze!" she called. "Wait! You're going too fast!"

The tiny brown owl flew back over to Willa Bean. "Apologies, *ma chérie*," he said. "I didn't realize you were so far behind."

Willa Bean and Snooze were on a short pajama flight before bed. The evening sky was a silvery blue color. Nimbus's nine clouds had already turned gold and pink around the edges. Pretty soon, it would be dark all over.

"I think I'm just too excited to fly fast tonight!" Willa Bean said. "My wings feel all wiggly!"

"What are you excited about?" Snooze asked.

Willa Bean shoved a curl out of her face. "Miss Twizzle is going to have a surprise for us in school tomorrow! And I can't wait to find out what it is!"

"How wonderful," said Snooze. "Surprises are marvelous things. What do you think it could be?"

Willa Bean stretched her wings out straight and glided next to Snooze. She liked to glide when she needed to think. Gliding made her brain work better. "Hmmm . . . ," she said. "Hmmm . . ."

Suddenly, she flapped her wings again.

"I know!" she said. "Maybe we're all getting brand-new quill pens!"

"That's quite possible," Snooze said. "A new quill pen would be a lovely surprise."

"But maybe not," Willa Bean said. "Especially since we just got new quill pens last week." She began to glide once more. "I know! Maybe Miss Twizzle has a big bag of Snoogy Bars for each of us! In every flavor!" Willa Bean giggled. "Wouldn't Harper go bonkers if that was the surprise?"

Harper was Willa Bean's best friend. She was crazy about Snoogy Bars.

"She would, indeed," Snooze said. "Harper loves Snoogy Bars, doesn't she?"

"Oh yes," Willa Bean said. "Especially peanut butter ones. One time, she ate twelve in a row! Without even stopping!"

"My goodness," Snooze said. "Didn't she get sick?"

"No." Willa Bean shook her head. "But she did get super thirsty."

"I don't know about Snoogy Bars, Willa Bean," Snooze said. "Do you think Miss Twizzle would hand out sweets in class?"

Willa Bean wrinkled her nose. "Maybe not."

"Well, keep on thinking," said Snooze. "But there's the North Star up ahead. We have to turn around."

Willa Bean looked into the distance. Snooze was right. The North Star was shining just above Cloud Eight, bright as a diamond. The silvery purple sky was getting darker, too. She turned around. So did Snooze.

In a few minutes, they were back at her bedroom window. Willa Bean flew inside her room. But as she landed, her foot slipped on a greasy spot. "Oof!" she said, falling to the floor. The seat of her pajamas turned mooshy and sticky.

"Willa Bean!" Snooze flew over and perched on her shoulder. "Are you all right? What happened?"

"I slipped on something." Willa Bean moved her bottom out of the gluey puddle. On the floor was a small, empty bottle. Without a cap.

"Oh *no*!" Willa Bean said. "Baby Louie got into my stardust paints! *Again!*" She stood up, holding the seat of her pajamas away from her. They were covered with sticky blue goo. "He dumped them all over the floor! Now my pajamas are ruined! And so are my paints!"

"Just the blue paint is ruined," Snooze pointed out. "All the other paint bottles look all right. And I'm sure your mother will be able to wash your pajamas."

Willa Bean stomped her foot. "I've told Baby Louie to stay out of my room! Prob'ly a million-bajillion times! And he never listens!"

"That's because he's a baby," Snooze

said. "Babies don't understand the things that big cupids do. They're too little."

Willa Bean stomped her foot again. "But it's not fair! Yesterday, he crawled into my closet and chewed my sandals! And then the other day, he tore the special picture I made for Mama in school! And now he's wrecked my jammies—and my blue stardust paint!" Willa Bean crossed her arms and stuck out her bottom lip. "I wish he would just go away! Forever!"

"You don't mean that." Snooze gave one of Willa Bean's curls a tug with his beak. "You love your little brother."

"I do not," Willa Bean said. "That baby is a Total Disaster. With a capital *T. D.*"

"Willa Bean!" Mama called from downstairs. "Time for bed!"

"I can't go to bed!" Willa Bean wailed. "I'm covered with paint!"

A short silence was followed by the sound of someone running upstairs. Then Daddy appeared in the bedroom doorway. "Willa Bean," he said, "did you just say you were . . ."

Willa Bean turned around.

". . . covered with paint?" Daddy stared at Willa Bean's pajama bottoms. "Oh dear. What happened?"

"Baby Louie dumped out my blue stardust paint." Willa Bean was trying not to cry. "And I slipped on it, and now it's a huge mess."

Daddy shook his head. "How many times have Mama and I told you not to leave your paints under your bed? Baby Louie is crawling everywhere now. And when he sees something on the floor—"

"But I forgot!" Willa Bean said.

"Okay." Daddy picked up the rest of the

paints. He set them on top of Willa Bean's dresser. "Let's keep them up here from now on, all right?"

Willa Bean sniffed and nodded.

Daddy held out his hand. "Come on, little love," he said. "We're going to have to get you in the shower. Mama will have a fit if she finds out you've gone to bed with a blue bottom."

"But I don't want to take a shower!" Willa Bean hung back. "I hate showers!"

"You hate washing your hair," Daddy reminded her. "You don't have to get your hair wet. Or even your face. Just the blue part." He grinned. "I don't think I know too many cupids out there with purple wings, brown hair, and blue bottoms."

Willa Bean wrinkled her nose. "It's not funny," she said.

Just then, Mama came into the room.

She was holding Baby Louie on her hip. "Everything okay here?" she asked.

Willa Bean looked at her baby brother. He was shoving Babyflakes into his mouth with one hand. In his other hand was his red rubber star-bubble ball. It was his most favorite toy in the universe. Baby Louie never let his red rubber star-bubble ball out of his sight. He even slept with it.

"No," Willa Bean said. "Baby Louie just wrecked my paints. And now I have a blue bottom, and I have to take a shower, and Daddy thinks it's funny!" She stomped off to the bathroom and shut the door behind her.

But not before she heard Baby Louie say, "Dunny!"

Baby Louie liked to repeat the last word Willa Bean said. Even if it didn't make any sense.

He was definitely a super-pest.

But he was not a super-smart one.

Chapter 2

Cloudtrip!

Willa Bean felt much better the next morning, especially when she remembered what day it was. In no time at all, she would be in school. And then she would find out Miss Twizzle's surprise!

After the cloudbus dropped them off, Willa Bean skipped into Class A. She stopped short and stared at the chalkboard. She mouthed the word on the board silently to herself. Then she jumped up and down and ran over to Harper. "Harper!

Harper! Look at the board! I think it's the surprise that Miss Twizzle told us about!"

Harper was busy putting her books inside her desk. But she turned around to look at the board. She squinted her eyes behind her blue polka-dotted glasses. She blinked a few times and then squinted some more.

"Hold on." Willa Bean stuck out her hand. "Your glasses have Snoogy Bar smudges all over them. I'll clean them for you."

Harper gave Willa Bean her glasses. Willa Bean rubbed the glass part very carefully on the bottom of her uniform. First one, then the other. Willa Bean was a super glass-cleaner.

When she was done, she gave Harper her glasses back. "Here," Willa Bean said. "They should be good and sparkly now."

Harper put her glasses back on. She blinked a few more times. "Ooooh," she said. "That's nice."

"Now you can read what's on the board!" Willa Bean said.

"Cloud. Trip." Harper said the parts of the word slowly. She looked at Willa Bean. Her eyes were very round. "A cloudtrip!" she said again. "Wizzle-dizzle-doodad, Willa Bean! A real cloudtrip? Do you think that's for us?"

Vivi pushed her way in between Willa Bean and Harper. "Of course it's for us. It's written on *our* chalkboard. Who else would it be for?" She fixed the big velvet bow in her red hair. "And guess what else? I heard Miss Twizzle talking to Mr. Rightflight about it yesterday. And so *I'm* the only one who knows where we're going on our cloudtrip."

Vivi sat down at her desk. It was right in front of Willa Bean's. Sitting near Vivi was not something Willa Bean was all that thrilled about. Especially since it meant Vivi could turn around in her seat and see everything Willa Bean did. It also meant she usually tattled to Miss Twizzle about it.

Sophie ran over to them. "You know where we're going on our cloudtrip, Vivi?" she asked. "For real?"

Vivi nodded. "I know *exactly* where we're going." She put her pink wingsack on her desk. It was covered with purple moondust glitter. A pink rubber star-bubble ball dangled from the zipper. Vivi took out her books and put them in her desk.

"Tell us!" Willa Bean begged. "Please!"

"Yeah!" Sophie said. "It's not fair that you're the only cupid who knows! We should *all* know, since we're *all* going!"

But Vivi shook her head. "I can't tell," she said. "Otherwise, Miss Twizzle will think I spied on her. When actually I really didn't. I just heard by accident when I came back to get my singing book."

"We won't tell." Willa Bean leaned in super-close to Vivi. "We promise."

Harper scooched in next to Willa Bean. So did Sophie. All three cupids stared at

Vivi, waiting to hear what she would say next.

But just then, the second bell rang.

Willa Bean turned around quickly. When the second bell rang, they were supposed to be in their seats. Miss Twizzle was coming into the classroom. Class would start any minute now.

Willa Bean grabbed her wingsack. She hurried over to her desk and put her books inside. Then she sat down.

"All right, class!" Miss Twizzle shut the door behind her and clapped her hands. "Everyone should be in their seats with their wings folded neatly!"

Willa Bean folded her purple wings neatly against her back. She sat up tall. She hoped Miss Twizzle noticed that she was in her seat. Even if her legs were wiggling and dancing under the desk.

Miss Twizzle waited. Her blond hair looked very shiny under the bright lights. Her eight freckles gleamed on her cheeks. Willa Bean thought Miss Twizzle was the most beautiful teacher she had ever seen.

Harper raised her hand.

"Yes, Harper?" Miss Twizzle asked.

"Is that *cloudtrip* word on the board for us?" Harper asked.

Miss Twizzle smiled. "It most certainly is," she said. "Tomorrow, Mr. Rightflight and I are taking all of you on your very first cloudtrip!"

Excited gasps filled the room.

Willa Bean wiggled up and down in her seat. Her desk bumped into the back of Vivi's chair. Vivi turned around. She frowned at Willa Bean.

"Sorry," Willa Bean whispered. "It was an accident."

Pedro, who sat in front of Raymond, jumped out of his chair. He pumped the air with his fist and did a little crazy dance with his feet. "Yessssss!" he shouted. "I *love* cloudtrips!"

Everyone in Class A laughed. Willa Bean laughed the loudest. Pedro cracked her up. He was a goofy cupid.

"Where are we *going* on our cloudtrip, Miss Twizzle?" Sophie asked. "Can you tell us? Please?"

"Of course I can tell you," Miss Twizzle said. "Mr. Rightflight and I are taking all of you to Cloud Nine."

Cloud Nine! Holy shamoley! Willa Bean had never been to Cloud Nine before! Not once! Her knees hopped and skipped with excitement. The front of her desk bumped into Vivi's chair again.

"Miss Twizzle!" Vivi called out. "Miss

Twizzle! Willa Bean keeps shoving her desk against my chair! And it is very annoying to me because I can't concentrate!"

Miss Twizzle looked at Willa Bean. "I know you're excited," she said. "But you have to try to sit still, Willa Bean."

Willa Bean nodded. Then, when Miss Twizzle turned back around, Willa Bean made a googly face at Vivi.

"Miss Twizzle!" Vivi called. "Willa Bean just made a googly face at me! Which is not listening to the Cupid Rule at all!"

Miss Twizzle sighed. She looked at Vivi for a moment. Then she looked at Willa Bean. "One more problem between you two," she said, "and I am going to have to send letters home to both of your parents."

Willa Bean sat very still. So did Vivi. Having a letter sent home was not a good thing. Not even a little bit.

"All right now." Miss Twizzle began to walk up and down between the desks. "Does anyone know what is *on* Cloud Nine?"

"Waterworld!" Class A shouted.

"That's exactly right," Miss Twizzle said. "So tomorrow we are all going to get very, very wet!"

Class A hollered and clapped.

"Cloud Nine also has a small area where you can practice using your bows and arrows," Miss Twizzle went on. "Mr. Rightflight would like to take everyone there first. When that's finished, we will head over to Waterworld. And you can swim and play for the rest of the day!"

"YAY!" Class A shouted.

"This is so cool!" Pedro jumped out of his chair again. This time, he did a little jiggly dance with his bottom. He shook his head from side to side and made his eyes all big and googly.

Willa Bean laughed again. She clapped her hands and wiggled up and down.

She felt exactly the same way.

Chapter 3

A Baby Blare!

"Mama! Mama!" Willa Bean called as she burst into the house after school. "Guess where we're going tomorrow? Guess where we're going?"

"I'm out here, sweetie!" Mama called.

Willa Bean followed Mama's voice. There was another voice, too. It sounded a lot like Baby Louie's. Except it was the slightest bit louder.

Mama was in the backyard. She was bouncing Baby Louie up and down on her

23

hip. "Shhh, my darling," she said. "It's okay. Shhh."

But Baby Louie wasn't listening. He was making the worst sound that Willa Bean had ever heard. It was a yell and a scream and a baby cry—all rolled up into one. It was a Baby Blare!

Willa Bean put her hands over her ears. "What's the matter with him?" she yelled.

"I can't find his red rubber star-bubble ball!" Mama hollered back. "He was playing with it this morning, and now it's gone!" She looked hopefully at Willa Bean. "You haven't seen it, have you?"

Willa Bean shook her head. "Nope," she said. Who cared about goofy old red rubber star-bubble balls anyway? They were boring. The only things rubber star-bubble balls could do were roll or bounce. Sometimes the baby stars inside them glowed,

but they didn't always work. Willa Bean
had a purple rubber star-bubble ball once.
But that was when she was a baby.

"Guess where we're going tomorrow?"

Willa Bean tried again. "On a cloudtrip! A real one! And guess which cloud we're going to?"

Mama looked exasperated. "In a minute, Willa Bean," she said. "Please help me look for Louie's star-bubble ball first. Maybe you'll think of a place that I haven't thought of yet."

Baby Louie stared at Willa Bean. For a brief second, he was quiet. His little eyes were red and swollen. His nose was running terribly, and he had drool coming out of his mouth. He blinked once. Twice. Then he took a deep breath. Another Baby Blare burst out of his mouth.

"Staw baw!" Baby Louie screamed. "Staw baw!"

"We'll find your star ball," Mama said, stroking Baby Louie's head. "Willa Bean is going to help Mama look, and we'll find it."

But Willa Bean did not want to look for Baby Louie's red rubber star-bubble ball. She did not want to look for anything of his, really. She was still annoyed with her baby brother. Last night, he had ruined her blue stardust paint and given her a blue bottom. Plus, she'd had to take a shower. All because of him.

She put her hands over her ears again. "I can't help you look!" she said to Mama. "Miss Twizzle said we have to get our bow and arrows ready for our cloudtrip. I have to go find mine and clean them up. They have to be nice and sparkly."

Mama raised one of her eyebrows. "You can do that later, Willa Bean. Now I am not asking you to help me look for your baby brother's toy. I am *telling* you. Or there will be no cloudtrip tomorrow. *Any*where."

Willa Bean stamped her foot.

"You may stamp your foot all you like," Mama said. "That is not going to help things, either."

"But *I* don't know where it is!" Willa Bean wailed.

"I just want you to help me look," Mama said. "For twenty minutes. Then you can go get your bow and arrows ready."

"Hmph," Willa Bean said.

"*Right* now." Mama was using her stern voice. That meant that she wasn't messing around. "Ariel is already looking upstairs. I'm going to search the kitchen again. And I want you to look in the backyard."

"*Pooey,*" Willa Bean said.

But she said it very softly so that Mama could not hear her.

♥

Willa Bean looked all over the backyard for Baby Louie's red rubber star-bubble ball.

First, she looked under the blue lily plants in Mama's garden. But she did not find the red rubber star-bubble ball. She smelled one of the flowers. It smelled like rain. She picked it and put it in her hair.

Next, she looked in between the wing-berry bushes. But there was no red rubber star-bubble ball. She picked eleven wing-berries and ate them, one by one. They were red and soft and very sweet.

She looked in a pile of old cloudtoys in the sandbox. She used to play with the toys when she was little. But there was no red rubber star-bubble ball. She sat for a while and played with her old Moon Tune Doll. The doll didn't have any more hair. And she was missing an eyebrow. But she used to be one of Willa Bean's favorite toys.

Next, Willa Bean checked inside Ariel's old cloudhouse. She looked up and she looked down. She looked inside and she looked outside. No red rubber star-bubble ball there, either. She crept back inside the old cloudhouse. She pretended that she lived in it, the way she used to imagine

when she was little. Now it was cramped. Her wings were getting smooshed. She couldn't even fit her legs all the way inside!

"Willa Bean?" Mama called from the kitchen window. "Any luck?"

"Nope." Willa Bean crawled out of the cloudhouse. "It's not anywhere out here."

"Okay." Mama sounded sad. "Thanks for looking. Your twenty minutes are up. Come on in now. You can go get your bow and arrows ready."

Finally! Willa Bean dashed inside. Baby Louie was still screaming. His face was bright red. And his little nose was running even worse than before.

Willa Bean flew upstairs. She went into her room and shut the door.

Quiet, at last.

Chapter 4

Where Does a Missing Voice Go?

The next morning, Willa Bean woke up to a strange noise. It sounded like the air being squeezed out of a balloon. It was hoarse and wheezy and a little bit squeaky. She sat up in bed. Was it Snooze? Maybe he was sick again.

She got out from under the covers. But Snooze wasn't in her closet. She leaned out the window. The air was warm and soft. The sky was the color of Mama's blue lilies.

Snooze was just coming around the corner. His brown wings were spread wide. "*Bonjour,* Willa Bean!" Snooze said. "You're up early!"

Willa Bean waited for her owl to settle himself on the sill. "Snooze," she said, petting the feathers on his head, "do you hear that strange sound?"

Snooze cocked his head to the right. He cocked it to the left. "My goodness, I do," he said. "What in the world is that?"

"I don't know," Willa Bean said. "I thought it was you. I thought maybe you got sick again."

"I'm healthy as a horse," Snooze said. "I just flew back from Montana."

"What's Montana?" Willa Bean asked.

"It's in the United States of America,"

Snooze said. "Out West. Lots of beautiful rivers and mountains. A really lovely place."

There was a knock on Willa Bean's door. "Can I come in?" Daddy called.

"Okay!" said Willa Bean.

Daddy opened the door. He was holding Baby Louie in his arms. Baby Louie's eyes were even redder than yesterday. He leaned against Daddy's shoulder and sucked his thumb. Weird sounds were coming out of his nose and mouth.

"I wanted to make sure you were up, little love," Daddy said. "You don't want to be late for school."

But Willa Bean just stared at her baby brother. "What's wrong with Baby Louie?" she asked.

Daddy touched Baby Louie's cheek with his finger. "He cried himself to sleep last night," he said. "It took a long, long time. And now his voice is gone. He's completely hoarse."

"His voice is *gone*?" Willa Bean asked. She felt a twinge of sad feeling inside. Maybe she should have looked a little harder for that silly ball of his.

Daddy nodded. "It was hard for him to sleep without that red rubber star-bubble ball. I hope we find it soon. Otherwise, it's going to be another long day."

Suddenly, Willa Bean remembered what day it was. It was Class A's cloudtrip day! To Cloud Nine! She was going to practice with her bow and arrows! And then go to Waterworld!

"I hope you find his ball, too," Willa Bean said. "But I really have to get dressed now, Daddy. I have a huge day ahead of me. Plus, I have to pack my bathing suit."

"Make sure to brush that hair, too," Daddy said. "You don't want Mama going after it when you come downstairs."

Willa Bean got dressed super-quick. She zipped up the back of her red-and-white uniform. She tightened the laces on her sandals. She put her orange-and-white checkered bathing suit in her wingsack.

Then she brushed her purple wings with the silver tips. They were soft and fluffy. She brushed her hair, too. It was not

soft and fluffy. It boinged out all over the place.

Oh well. There was only so much a cupid could do in the morning. It was time to go. Her very first cloudtrip was waiting!

"Good-bye, Snooze!" Willa Bean kissed the top of her owl's head. "I'll tell you all about my trip when I get back."

"*Au revoir,*" Snooze said. His beak opened into a yawn. He rubbed his wide yellow eyes and shook out his tail feathers. "I'm just about ready for bed myself."

Willa Bean grabbed her wingsack and her bow and arrows and headed for the door. Then she stopped. "Snooze?" she said.

"Yes?" Snooze looked up.

"Where do you think Baby Louie's voice went?" Willa Bean asked.

"What do you mean?" said Snooze.

"Well, Daddy said it's gone," Willa Bean said. "Where do you think it went?"

"I think it's just plain tired out." Snooze flew over and settled himself on Willa Bean's shoulder. "And when it gets a good rest, it will come out of hiding again. Just like me."

Chapter 5

Polka-Dotted,

Silver-Knotted Arrow

One by one, Class A piled on the cloudbus.
Mr. Bibby, the cloudbus driver, was taking
them to Cloud Nine for their cloudtrip.

Willa Bean climbed the steps of the
cloudbus. She stopped when she reached
the last one. Mr. Bibby was wearing a black
bow tie today. It had white stripes on it.
"Your bow tie looks wonderful, Mr. Bibby!"
she said. "It matches your hair!"

"Thank you, Willa Bean," Mr. Bibby said. "And you certainly look like a grown-up cupid with your bow and arrows on your back!"

Willa Bean felt her inside proud feeling filling up. She wished she could take her real bow and arrows to school every day. But that wasn't the way Mr. Rightflight did things. He had boring old practice arrows for the cupids at school.

Today was different, though. Today was special. Everyone was allowed to bring their real, very own bows and arrows on the cloudtrip. Mr. Rightflight wanted them to use their own arrows when they practiced on Cloud Nine.

Their own arrows were very light. They weighed almost nothing at all. They had soft, squishy tips, too, which were covered with velvet. From far away, arrows looked as if they might hurt when cupids used them. But they didn't. In fact, they felt like little kisses.

Willa Bean took her favorite arrow from her quiver. It was silver with white polka dots. At the very bottom of the arrow was a special silver knot. The knot made the arrow go extra fast. She had spent a long time cleaning the arrow last night. Now it was shiny smooth. It sparkled in the sun.

"Look at this one, Mr. Bibby!" Willa Bean said. She held out her special arrow in front of him. "Mama and Daddy got it for me last year! For my birthday!"

"Willa Bean!" Miss Twizzle called out. "Keep moving, please. All the cupids behind you are waiting to get on the cloudbus, too."

"It's a magnificent arrow!" Mr. Bibby whispered. "I've never seen one like that! Now hurry back to your seat so we don't hold everyone up."

Willa Bean shoved her silver-knotted, polka-dotted arrow back in its quiver. She hopped down the middle of the cloudbus. Then she squeezed in next to Harper, who was eating a Snoogy Bar.

"Hi, Willa Bean!" Harper said. "You want some of my Snoogy Bar? It's a lemon wingberry!"

"No thanks," Willa Bean said. "I already had Wingfastic cereal for breakfast. I wanted to make sure I had extra energy this morning."

Vivi was sitting by herself in front of Willa Bean and Harper. She turned around and looked over the seat. "I saw you showing that silver-knotted, polka-dotted arrow to Mr. Bibby," she said. "Where did you get it?"

"My mama and daddy," Willa Bean said proudly. "They gave it to me last year. For my birthday. It's my most special arrow in the world." She hugged her quiver to her chest. Just to show that she meant it.

"I can't believe you have a real silver-knotted, polka-dotted arrow." Vivi's face looked mad. "That's not fair. My mom said that they're almost impossible to find. She still hasn't gotten me one."

"Oh well," Willa Bean said. "I guess that's just how it goes."

"Yeah." Vivi turned back around slowly. "I guess so." She put her wingsack on her lap and fiddled with her pink rubber star-bubble ball.

"Hey, Willa Bean!" At the back of the bus, Pedro and Raymond were waving their arms. "Bring your arrows over here! We want to see that really cool one!"

"I want to see it, too!" Sophie called.

"And me!" yelled Lola.

Willa Bean stood up. She would just run really quick to the back of the bus to show Pedro and Sophie and all the rest of the cupids. No one else had an extra-special silver-knotted, polka-dotted arrow except her!

But then she heard her name being called. Her real, super-long name. It was

the one that Mama used at home when she was not particularly pleased with Willa Bean.

"Wilhelmina Bernadina Skylight!" It was Miss Twizzle. "Mr. Bibby will not start this cloudbus until you are seated!"

Mr. Rightflight was standing next to Miss Twizzle. His silver whistle hung around his neck. He did not look very pleased, either.

Harper tugged on Willa Bean's sleeve. "Park it, lady!" she whispered. "Else we'll never get to Cloud Nine!"

Willa Bean sat down fast.

She clicked on her cloudbelt.

Very slowly, the cloudbus began to move. Class A was off on its very first cloudtrip!

Chapter 6

Cloud Nine Is Mighty Fine!

It did not take long to get to Cloud Nine. In fact, Willa Bean was just telling Harper about Baby Louie and his missing star-bubble ball when Mr. Rightflight stood up.

"All right, cupids!" he hollered from the front of the bus. "I need complete quiet!"

The buzz of cupid chatter stopped. Everyone looked at their flying teacher. Mr. Rightflight was not very tall. And he did not have much hair, especially in the front. But he had a very big voice. And he knew how to use it.

"We have arrived at Cloud Nine!" Mr. Rightflight boomed. "I need everyone to line up—quietly! Make sure that your quivers are buckled across the front of your chest, and that all your arrows are inside!"

Harper hopped up and down next to Willa Bean. "Check my arrows, will you, Willa Bean?" she asked.

Willa Bean peeked inside Harper's quiver. She had two orange arrows, two blue arrows, and three white ones. "Perfect," Willa Bean said. "Now can you check mine?"

Willa Bean turned around so Harper could see her arrows. She stood very still as Harper counted out loud. "Two orange, two blue, three white."

"And . . . ?" Willa Bean asked.

"And one silver-knotted, polka-dotted arrow!" Harper yelled.

"Woo-hoo!" Willa Bean hollered.

Suddenly, Mr. Rightflight appeared in front of Willa Bean and Harper. His arms were crossed over his chest. His mouth was turned upside down. "What part of 'quietly' do you cupids not understand?" he asked.

Willa Bean clapped her hand over her mouth. So did Harper.

Vivi tapped Mr. Rightflight on the sleeve. "Actually, they've been yelling during the whole trip," she said. "And now I have a headache."

"One more outburst back here," Mr. Rightflight said, "and both of you will stay on the bus while we practice."

Harper's eyes got very wide behind her blue polka-dotted glasses. She nodded. So did Willa Bean.

Mr. Rightflight looked at Willa Bean's quiver. "Where did you get this arrow?" He pointed to Willa Bean's silver-knotted, polka-dotted arrow.

Willa Bean shook her head. She pressed her hand against her mouth.

"Willa Bean," Mr. Rightflight said, "you can talk now. I just asked you a question."

Willa Bean dropped her hand away from her mouth. She took a gigantic breath. "I got it for my birthday last year," she said. "From Mama and Daddy."

"Well," Mr. Rightflight said, "it sure is a beauty. Those are hard to come by these days. You're a lucky little cupid."

Willa Bean nodded. "Actually," she said, "I think it's 'cause my parents adore me."

Mr. Rightflight coughed. Then he brought his silver whistle to his mouth and blew on it. "All right! Let's get moving here. Everyone off the bus!"

One by one, the cupids filed off the bus. Mr. Rightflight led them to a wide area dotted with small buildings and circled by

a fence. On the other side of the fence was
Waterworld!

Willa Bean stood on her tiptoes. Over
the top of the fence, she could see a bright
green slide. It was almost as high as a cloud!
And it had three upside-down loops in the
middle of it!

She tugged on Harper's sleeve. "Look at
the slide!" Willa Bean whispered.

"I'm already looking at it!" Harper said. "Wanna go down it together?"

Willa Bean nodded. She had hoped Harper would say that. Going down such a high slide seemed a little bit scary. Especially if it had upside-down loops in the middle of it.

Mr. Rightflight blew his whistle again. "Okay, cupids! Listen up! We are in the gift-shop area outside Waterworld, where you can buy gifts or cloudcandy on your way out of the park. Usually, these shops are open. But it's early, so everything is still closed. I want you to pretend that these shops are Earth buildings. And that Earth children are playing around them."

Miss Twizzle cleared her throat. "What's the most important thing cupids have to remember before they let an arrow fly?" she asked.

Lots of hands went up.

"Lola?" Miss Twizzle asked.

"To stay out of sight!" Lola shouted.

"That's exactly right," Mr. Rightflight said. "Earth children should never, ever see you when you release your arrow. Otherwise, it won't work."

"What's the second thing you need to remember?" Miss Twizzle asked.

"Always point your arrow at their feet!" Pedro yelled.

"Correct," Mr. Rightflight said. "Cupid arrows are extremely soft, so they won't hurt anyone. But you don't want to frighten an Earth child, either. If you shoot an arrow at their feet, they will just think they have tripped over a little twig. And they won't get scared."

Willa Bean tried to listen. She knew that what Mr. Rightflight was saying was important. But Vivi was standing in front of her. And so was her pink rubber star-bubble ball. It was dangling back and forth on the zipper of her wingsack.

Looking at Vivi's star-bubble ball made Willa Bean think about Baby Louie's lost star-bubble ball. She thought about her baby brother's puffy red eyes and super-runny nose. And then she remembered all the terrible wheezy sounds he had made that morning. Daddy said he had cried for a long, long time last night. And now his voice was gone!

Willa Bean reached over and tapped on Vivi's shoulder.

Vivi turned around. She made a mad face at Willa Bean. *"What?"* she whispered.

"Why do you have a rubber star-bubble ball?" Willa Bean whispered. "Aren't those just for babies?"

Vivi wrinkled her nose. "You're supposed to be paying *attention,* Willa Bean. And for your information, my rubber star-bubble ball was a special present from my grandmother. She went to heaven when I was little. So I still keep it 'cause it makes me think of her."

Willa Bean blinked. "Oh," she said. "Does it still glow?"

"Mr. Rightflight!" Vivi yelled. "Mr. Rightflight! Willa Bean keeps on talking to me! And it's very annoying, because I can't pay attention to what you are telling us!"

Miss Twizzle walked over. She took Willa Bean by the hand and led her away from the group. She made Willa Bean stand right next to her. Then she leaned down and whispered in her ear, "You must pay attention, Willa Bean. This is very important."

Willa Bean stood up straight. She told herself not to think about Baby Louie. Or Vivi's pink rubber star-bubble ball. She listened to Mr. Rightflight. It was not a hard thing to do. He was talking very loudly.

"Okay," Mr. Rightflight said. "I think we're ready. Half of you are going to pretend to be Earth children. And the other half will practice with your arrows."

"I want to shoot my arrows first!" Vivi screamed. "Let me, Mr. Rightflight! Please!"

"And me!" yelled Pedro.

"I want to, too!" shouted Lola.

"Calm down, everyone," said Mr. Rightflight. "You will all get a chance to shoot your arrows. Everyone will also get a chance to pretend to be an Earth child. That's the whole reason we're here."

Willa Bean was in the cupid group that was going to shoot arrows first. So was Harper.

By now, Baby Louie was way far back in her brain. So was Vivi's pink rubber starbubble ball.

It was time to get down to business.

Chapter 7

A Super Gift Store!

Willa Bean stayed close to Harper as they crept toward the gift shops. She could hear other cupids yelling and shouting. They were pretending to be Earth children. Willa Bean held her bow and arrow close and crept around one of the buildings.

Up close, the gift shops looked much bigger. They had signs on the front doors.

One of them said WATERWORLD POSTCARDS. Postcards were boring. Willa Bean tiptoed past it quickly.

The next one said WATERWORLD SHOES & CLOTHES. Willa Bean didn't have any clothing from Waterworld. Maybe Mama would get her a Waterworld bathing suit next year.

The one after that said GOLDEN ARROWS. Willa Bean's eyes turned wide when she saw that one. Golden arrows were only used by big cupids. Mama and Daddy had golden arrows. Daddy used them every day when he went down to Earth to help big people fall in love. Golden arrows were very, very special.

"Willa Bean!" Harper whispered. "Come here! Look!"

Willa Bean ran toward her. Harper pointed to another gift shop, a little farther away. The sign on the door said WATERWORLD WING FEATHERS.

"So?" Willa Bean asked.

"Underneath!" Harper pointed. "Look what it says underneath!"

Willa Bean crept closer. And there, underneath WATERWORLD WING FEATHERS, were three more words. "Waterworld Snoogy Bars!" Willa Bean squealed.

"Lolly-dolly-doodad!" Harper yelled. "Can you imagine? A whole entire gift store full of Snoogy Bars!" She did three twirls. "It's like my secret dream come true!"

Willa Bean giggled.

But she stopped giggling when Vivi marched over. "You two better stop fooling around," Vivi said. "Else I'm going back and telling Mr. Rightflight that you're distracting the rest of us."

"Oh pooey!" Willa Bean said. "You're not the boss of us, Vivi!"

"Well, Mr. Rightflight is." Vivi tossed

her head. "And so is Miss Twizzle. And if I go back and tell them what you're doing, you'll have to sit on the bus for the rest of the day! So there!"

"Come on." Harper took Willa Bean's hand. "Vivi's right. We have to pay attention. Else we'll never get this right."

Vivi flounced off. Raymond, Hannah, Pedro, and Sophie followed her. They moved on tiptoes. They looked for places to hide. Willa Bean and Harper did, too. The shouts of the other cupids were getting louder. It was almost time to use their arrows.

"I can't stand that old Vivi," Willa Bean whispered to Harper. "She is turning my life into a crazy-daisy!"

"What's a crazy-daisy?" Harper asked.

"I'm not sure." Willa Bean shrugged. "I just made it up."

Harper thought about that as they walked. "I like it," she said. "It rhymes."

Willa Bean nodded. "Here's another one," she said. "A loopy-poopy!"

Harper laughed. "How about a wacky-dacky?"

"Or a . . ." Willa Bean stopped short. Right in front of another gift shop. "Holy shamoley," she said.

"I like *holy shamoley,* too," Harper said. "Except you say that one a lot."

"No!" Willa Bean pointed to the gift shop. "I meant *holy shamoley!* Look!"

Harper looked at the gift shop, too. The sign on the front door said WATERWORLD TOYS, ETC. in big black letters.

"Do you know what's in there?" Willa Bean asked Harper.

"Yeah," Harper said. "Toys! And Etc.!"

"Right." Willa Bean looked at Harper.

"We have to get inside," she whispered. "Just for an eensy-weensy, teeny-tiny second."

Harper's eyes turned wide. "No way, Willa Bean! We're not allowed to go *inside* the gift shops! We just have to hide *behind* them! So the other cupids don't see us!"

Willa Bean shook her head. "We'll be super-quick."

"We can't!" Harper looked scared now. She took a step back. "Mr. Rightflight said! We'll get in trouble."

"Okay," Willa Bean said. "You just stand watch, then. To make sure no one sees me. I'll go in by myself."

"But why do you have to go in at all?" Harper asked.

"Because of those!" Willa Bean had already flown up to the window at the top of the gift shop. Harper flew up next to her. The cupids peeked inside. Willa Bean pointed to one corner.

"Ohhhh!" Harper said.

Willa Bean smiled. "See?" she said. "That's why I have to go in!"

Harper looked again at the enormous white bucket in the corner.

It was filled to the top with red rubber star-bubble balls.

Chapter 8

Upside Down

and Inside Out

The window was open a little bit at the top. It was just enough so that Willa Bean thought she could squeeze through.

Harper stood on guard next to the gift shop, looking all around. She tapped the sides of her glasses with her fingers. Harper did a lot of glasses-tapping when she was nervous.

"Is anybody watching?" Willa Bean whispered.

Harper checked behind her. She looked to the right and then to the left. "Nope!" she called up to Willa Bean. "But hurry!"

"I will!" Willa Bean tried to stick her head through the window crack. But her hair was too wide. It got in the way—all over the place!

She tried to push the window open a little wider. But it was too heavy. She pushed and pushed. It didn't even budge an inch.

Next, she tried smooshing her hair down on the sides. She used both hands and pressed down super-hard. Then she tried to squeeze through the window again. But now her elbows got in the way!

"Pooey!" Willa Bean said. She stared at the window crack for a moment. She thought and thought. "I know!" she said suddenly. She turned around. And then she wiggled her feet through the crack. They went in! So did her knees! And her wings! And her shoulders, too!

But when it came time for her hair to go in, Willa Bean stopped moving. There was simply too much of it. It stuck fast in the window. It was being very stubborn.

Again, Willa Bean thought and thought.

She moved her head to the right. Then she moved her head to the left. Slowly, slowly, her hair began to slide through the crack. She kept moving her head. Right. Left. Right. Left. All of a sudden, with a great whooshing sound, it came unstuck! Willa Bean was inside the gift shop!

She blinked a few times. It was very dark in there. Even with the window open, it was hard to see. Willa Bean felt nervous inside. She would have to move quickly.

She was not a big fan of dark places.

A huge pile of rubber baby dolls sat in one corner. They were wearing Waterworld bathing suits. Next to the dolls were plastic slides, and toy trumpets, and even a blue rocking sea horse! Willa Bean tried to ignore the toys, but it was impossible.

She went over and sat on the sea horse. She had never been on one before. She had never even *seen* one before! She rocked back and forth. She leaned forward and pretended she was in a race, riding a real racehorse. Snooze had told her about racehorses before. He had watched a real, live horse race in Paris!

Willa Bean pretended she had a helmet on her head. Her feet were in the stirrups. She held the reins tightly in her hand. She clicked with her mouth just like Snooze told her real riders did.

"Let's go, Mr. Blue!" she said. "We're gonna win this race!"

Willa Bean pretended other horses were around her and Mr. Blue. To her right was a cream-colored one. To her left was a black horse with a white star on his forehead. But Mr. Blue was the fastest. Back and forth Willa Bean rocked. Faster and faster, until . . . *BAM!*

Willa Bean found herself on the ground. Mr. Blue was still rocking. Willa Bean got to her feet. What a ride! She would try again. This time she wouldn't fall off. This time, she would stay on Mr. Blue until the end and come in first!

She started to get back on. But then she saw the white bucket in the corner. Willa Bean sighed. Slowly, she slid off Mr. Blue. Now was no time to be playing around. She was down here for one thing, and one thing only.

She stepped over to the white bucket. She picked out the roundest, reddest, rubberiest star-bubble ball she could find. Then she stuck it in her pocket and flew back up to the window.

Willa Bean tried to wiggle through the window. But her hair had decided to be stubborn again. It made her stuck. She turned herself upside down. But her wings did not work when she was upside down. They only worked when she was right side up. Maybe they did not know how yet. Or maybe they were just confused.

Being upside down could confuse anyone.

Willa Bean put her mouth against the window crack. "Harper!" She made her voice into a whisper-scream. "Harper! Are you still there?"

There was no answer.

Willa Bean tried again. She made her voice a little bit louder than a whisper-scream. "Harper! It's me! Fly up to the window again, okay? I need you!"

There was a noise down below. Willa Bean turned around. The noise was coming from behind the front door. "Willa Bean!" Harper whispered.

Willa Bean smiled and flew back down to the ground. Harper was such a good friend. She was always there to help Willa Bean. Sometimes Willa Bean didn't even have to ask for what she needed. Harper just knew. She was the best friend in the entire universe.

Willa Bean ran toward the door. Harper would be so happy when she saw what she had found! She would laugh and clap her hands. Maybe she could even come with Willa Bean after school to give it to Baby Louie.

The front door swung open.

There was Harper.

And Vivi, and Raymond, and Sophie, and all the rest of the cupids.

Mr. Rightflight was there.

And Miss Twizzle, too.

No one was laughing. Or clapping their hands.

Not even a little bit.

Chapter 9

Time-Out

Willa Bean gulped when she saw everyone standing there. Especially Mr. Rightflight. And Miss Twizzle. She tried to smile. But her lips did not move the right way. Her smile came out all wibbly-wobbly. So she did a little wave instead.

"Hi, everyone!" Willa Bean said. "I'm very glad you're here. Because if you weren't, I would still be stuck!"

"Willa Bean Skylight," Miss Twizzle said. "Come with me this instant."

Willa Bean took a step forward.

"Miss Twizzle!" Vivi called. "Miss Twizzle! Willa Bean has something in her pocket! And I don't think it's supposed to be there!"

Willa Bean clapped her hand over her pocket.

Now Mr. Rightflight came forward. "Please take your hand off your pocket, Willa Bean," he said.

Willa Bean took her hand away from her pocket.

One.

Finger.

At.

A.

Time.

"Now," Mr. Rightflight said, "put your hand inside your pocket, take out what's in there, and give it to me."

Willa Bean slid her hand inside her pocket. She felt around. Then she pulled out a small, flat moonstone. It was orange. She had found it yesterday, on her way home from school. She held the moonstone out to Mr. Rightflight.

Mr. Rightflight's eye twitched. "Not the moonstone, Willa Bean," he said.

Willa Bean put the moonstone back inside her pocket. She felt around once more. This time, she pulled out a piece of purple felt ribbon. She had found the ribbon on Moonday. It was going to go into the treasure chest she and Harper shared, along with the moonstone.

"Willa Bean." Miss Twizzle was tapping her fingertips together. "Do not make Mr. Rightflight ask you again. Give him the *round thing* that is in your pocket."

Willa Bean looked at Vivi. "You are the

biggest, meanest, tattletale-est cupid in Nimbus!" she yelled. "That's why no one wants to be your friend! Or even sit with you on the cloudbus when we have cloud-trips!"

"That is enough, Willa Bean!" Mr. Rightflight's voice was very stern. His hand was still outstretched, waiting.

Willa Bean reached into her pocket. She pulled out the red rubber star-bubble ball and handed it to Mr. Rightflight.

"Thank you," Mr. Rightflight said. He gave the red rubber star-bubble ball to Miss Twizzle, who put it back in the white bucket.

"Come with me, Willa Bean," Miss Twizzle said. "Since you did not follow the rules, you are going to have to spend the rest of the cloudtrip on the bus."

"You mean I can't go to Waterworld?" Willa Bean cried.

Miss Twizzle shook her head. "I'm sorry, Willa Bean."

Willa Bean took Miss Twizzle's hand. It was warm and soft, but she hardly even noticed. Mostly because her inside crying feeling was starting up. She bit her tongue. She did not want to cry in front of all the other cupids. Especially that mean old tattletale Vivi.

Miss Twizzle led her toward the cloudbus. Behind her, Willa Bean could hear Mr. Rightflight yelling. "All right, cupids! Let's get back to bow-and-arrow practice!"

Willa Bean sniffed.

And then she sniffed again.

There was a big, round pain in the back of her throat. She tried to swallow over it. But it just got bigger. And by the time she got to the bus, it hurt so much that she opened her mouth.

A long, sad cry came out.

Miss Twizzle sat down in the seat next to her. She let Willa Bean cry for a few minutes. Then she gave her a green tissue. Willa Bean pressed it to her nose. She blew into it until her nose felt better. Her eyes were dry again, too. But she did not feel good inside. Not even a little bit.

"May I ask you a question, Willa Bean?" Miss Twizzle asked finally.

Willa Bean nodded.

"Why did you go inside that gift shop?"
Miss Twizzle asked.

Willa Bean picked at the edge of her
seat. She did not answer.

"I believe what Mr. Rightflight told you to do," Miss Twizzle went on, "was to sneak around them. Or fly over them. He did not say to go inside. Not once."

"I know," Willa Bean whispered.

"And then you took something that did not belong to you," Miss Twizzle said. "That is not allowed, no matter where we go. Ever."

"I know," Willa Bean whispered again.

Miss Twizzle sighed. "Besides, if you really want a rubber star-bubble ball that much, I'm sure your parents would get you one."

"But it wasn't for me!" Willa Bean burst out. "I don't even *like* rubber star-bubble balls! I think they're boring! It was for Baby Louie! He loves them even more than Babyflakes! His red star-bubble ball is his most favorite thing in the whole entire uvinerse. He even sleeps with it. And yesterday he lost it. And he's been crying ever since. He cried so hard last night that he lost his voice, Miss Twizzle! His own little baby voice! It's gone!"

"Ah," Miss Twizzle said slowly. "I see."

Willa Bean stared out the window. It was hard to see since her eyes were wet with tears again. Everything looked blurry and smeared. She took a deep, shuddery breath.

"Let me ask you something else," Miss Twizzle said gently. "How do you think Vivi felt after you said those things to her? About not having any friends? And sitting alone on the bus during our cloudtrip?"

Willa Bean twirled a piece of her hair around her finger. She knew the things she said were mean. But Vivi just made her so mad. She drove Willa Bean into a crazy-daisy with all the tattling she did!

"I know Vivi can be difficult some-times," Miss Twizzle said.

"She tells on me!" Willa Bean said. "No matter what I do! She just tattles and tat-tles!"

Miss Twizzle nodded. "I've noticed that," she said. "I've also noticed that Vivi seems to think very highly of you."

"You mean . . ." Willa Bean paused. "You think she *likes* me?"

"I think she likes you a great deal," Miss Twizzle said. "And I don't think she knows how to tell you that."

Willa Bean thought about this for a moment. It sounded nice, but she wasn't sure it made very much sense. Why would someone who liked her tattle on her all the time?

"Think about Baby Louie for just a

moment," Miss Twizzle said. "Does he ever get on your nerves?"

Willa Bean nodded. "All the time."

"Is he ever a pest?" Miss Twizzle asked.

Willa Bean almost laughed. "Every day."

"I would bet my wings that what he really wants is to spend time with you. He probably thinks you're the greatest thing in the world, Willa Bean. But he doesn't know how to tell you that. So he acts like a pest instead, to try to get your attention. Maybe the same is true for Vivi."

Willa Bean looked out the window again. She wondered how Miss Twizzle knew so much about everything.

"I want you to listen carefully to me, Willa Bean." Miss Twizzle's voice was very soft. "It's very, very lovely of you to be so kind to your baby brother. But you broke several very important rules. You didn't listen to Mr. Rightflight. You took something that didn't belong to you. And you broke the Cupid Rule when you were mean to Vivi. So you are going to have to stay on the bus with me for one hour. After that, I will take you to Waterworld."

"A whole hour?" Willa Bean said.

"It's that or nothing," Miss Twizzle said.

Willa Bean sat back in her seat. She thought about the Cupid Rule:

The very best way
To spend your day
Is to try to be kind—
All the time.

Why were some rules so hard to follow?

And why did there have to be so many of them in the first place?

Chapter 10

Let's Trade

Willa Bean sat quietly on the bus, exactly the way Miss Twizzle told her to do. It was incredibly boring. Miss Twizzle sat up front, reading a book. But Willa Bean did not have any books with her. And it was going to be a whole hour before she could leave again. That was like forever!

She lay down on her seat and stared up at the ceiling. She raised her feet over her head and wiggled her toes inside her sandals.

She had cute little toes. She liked them very much.

She pressed her nose against the window. She made little huffy breaths with her mouth and drew pictures in the foggy part of the window.

She drew a picture of Snooze flying. Then she drew a picture of Snooze sitting still. She drew Harper with her glasses on. Then she drew Harper with her glasses off. She drew a picture of her silver-knotted, polka-dotted arrow in her quiver. Then she drew a picture of it flying through the air.

She took her silver-knotted, polka-dotted arrow out of her quiver. She ran her fingers over the smooth silver. Slowly, she counted all the polka dots. There were seventeen of them!

"All right, Willa Bean," Miss Twizzle said. "Time's up. Let's go to Waterworld!"

Willa Bean jumped up and down. She did not walk next to Miss Twizzle. She flew! As fast as she could! In two seconds, she was inside Waterworld. She changed quickly into her orange bathing suit and ran to join Class A. They were all standing next to the big green slide. Willa Bean shouted and wiggled her wings. She was so happy to see everyone again.

Well, almost everyone.

"Willa Bean!" Harper yelled. "You're back!" She hugged her best friend. "I missed you. Are you all right?"

"Yes!" Willa Bean jumped up and down. "But I'm so glad I'm back! It was boring on the bus without you!"

For the next hour, the cupids flew all over Waterworld. They went on the green slide with the three upside-down loops. They splashed around in the big blue pool

with stars on the bottom. They rode the river rapids in big, fat moontubes. And they went into the super-duper wave-cave, where it was dark and scary! By the time it was all over, Willa Bean was grinning from ear to ear!

Later, on the cloudbus, Vivi sat alone again. She was very quiet. In fact, Willa Bean couldn't remember Vivi saying any-thing during any of the Waterworld rides. Or even on the walk back to the cloudbus.

And then, as the cloudbus started, Vivi turned around. She got up on her knees and held out her pink rubber star-bubble ball to Willa Bean. "I want you to have this," Vivi said. "For Baby Louie."

Willa Bean stared at the ball. Then she stared at Vivi. "How'd you know about Baby Louie?" she asked.

"Harper told me after you got sent back to the bus," Vivi said. "She said that was the whole reason you went into the gift shop. So you could get a star-bubble ball for your little brother." Vivi's lower lip quivered. "And then I went and ruined it by tattling on you." She pushed the ball into Willa Bean's hands. "Here. I want you to have it."

Willa Bean took Vivi's pink rubber star-bubble ball. Vivi turned around super-quick. She sat back down. Her wings shook. Little sniffing sounds came out of her mouth.

"Toodle-noodle-bing-bang!" whispered Harper. "How about *that*?"

Willa Bean sat very still. She thought about what Miss Twizzle had said to her on the bus. She looked at Vivi sitting by herself. And then she looked down at the star-bubble ball in her hands. Willa Bean did not say anything. Her stomach was doing flip-flops.

Willa Bean reached for something on the seat. Then she tapped Vivi on the shoulder.

Vivi turned around. "Yes?" she asked.

Willa Bean opened her mouth. But nothing came out.

"What, Willa Bean?" Vivi asked. "Are you playing a trick on me?"

Willa Bean shook her head. She lifted up her silver-knotted, polka-dotted arrow.

"I already know you have a special arrow," Vivi said. "You don't have to rub it in."

"I don't want to rub it in." Willa Bean's voice was a little squeak. "I want to do a trade."

"A trade?" Vivi repeated.

Willa Bean nodded. "I'll trade you my arrow for your pink rubber star-bubble ball."

"No, Willa Bean!" Harper tugged on Willa Bean's sleeve. "Don't do that! That's your most favorite arrow!"

But Willa Bean stared straight ahead. This was something she wanted to do, even if she didn't know how to say it right.

Vivi blinked. She looked at Harper. Then she looked back at Willa Bean. "Are you just trying to be funny?" she asked.

Willa Bean shook her head. "Nope." She held out the arrow.

Vivi took the arrow. She ran her fingers over it. She touched the silver knot at the end very lightly. And she counted all the polka dots.

Willa Bean sat back in her seat. Her quiver already felt different. Lighter. And so did a little, tiny part of her. Especially when she thought how happy Baby Louie would be when he saw the rubber ball.

But the other, bigger part of her felt sad. She would miss her favorite arrow terribly. And as the cloudbus swung around

Cloud Nine and headed for home, Willa Bean put her head down on her knees and tried not to cry.

That night, Mama and Daddy and Ariel and Willa Bean watched as Baby Louie played with his new pink rubber star-bubble ball. His eyes were wide and bright. His cheeks were flushed a soft rosy color. He made happy googly noises with his mouth and clapped his hands. Willa Bean felt very happy, watching him. It almost made her forget about her special arrow.

Just then, a knock came at the door.

Daddy went to answer it. "Miss Twizzle!" he said, opening the door wide. "How nice to see you! Come in!"

Willa Bean jumped up. She ran behind the couch and tried to make herself invisible. She hadn't told Mama and Daddy about all the trouble she had gotten into on her cloudtrip. Was Miss Twizzle going to tell them that Willa Bean had misbehaved? And that she'd had to sit on the cloudbus for a whole hour?

Willa Bean peeked out from behind the couch. Miss Twizzle had something in her hand. It looked like an arrow. In fact, it looked like *her* arrow.

"I just want you to know," Miss Twizzle said, "that two of my students did something marvelous today." She smiled. "Willa Bean was one of them. She traded her favorite arrow for a rubber star-bubble ball, so that she could give it to her baby brother."

"Willa Bean," Mama said softly, "I had no idea. I thought you had an extra rubber ball in your treasure chest."

"I know how much this means to you," Miss Twizzle said. She held out the silver-knotted, polka-dotted arrow and looked at Willa Bean. "That's why I'm returning it."

Willa Bean jumped out from behind the couch. She ran over to her teacher and took her favorite arrow in her hands.

"That's very kind of you, Miss Twizzle," Daddy said. "Thank you so much."

"You're very welcome," Miss Twizzle

said. "But I'm also here to get Vivi's rubber ball back. It was a gift from her grandmother. And I know it means a lot to her, as well."

"But . . ." Willa Bean looked at Baby Louie. He was still drooling all over that pink ball.

"Don't worry." Miss Twizzle reached into her pocket and pulled out a red rubber star-bubble ball. "I bought this one at Waterworld today for this very reason."

Willa Bean stared at her teacher. She didn't know how Miss Twizzle did everything the way she did. It was almost impossible to say how wonderful she was. Instead, Willa Bean threw her arms around her. She hugged her very hard.

Baby Louie didn't even notice when they switched the balls. He laughed and clapped some more. And then he did a big baby burp.

Everyone laughed.

Willa Bean held her silver-knotted, polka-dotted arrow tight and watched her baby brother play with his new ball.

It had been a hard day with all its ups and downs.

But, she thought, she wouldn't trade it for anything.